WHERE IS BEAR?

JONATHAN BENTLEY

LITTLE HARE
www.littleharebooks.com

Where is Bear?

Where could Bear be?

Is Bear in the drawer?

Is Bear on the shelf?

Where is Bear?

I saw him somewhere.
But where?

In the bathroom?

Downstairs?

Is Bear on the table?

Is Bear under the sofa?

Where is Bear?

Where could Bear be?

On the swing?

In the car?

I just don't know.
I'm getting tired.

I want to sleep, so ...

WHERE IS BEAR?

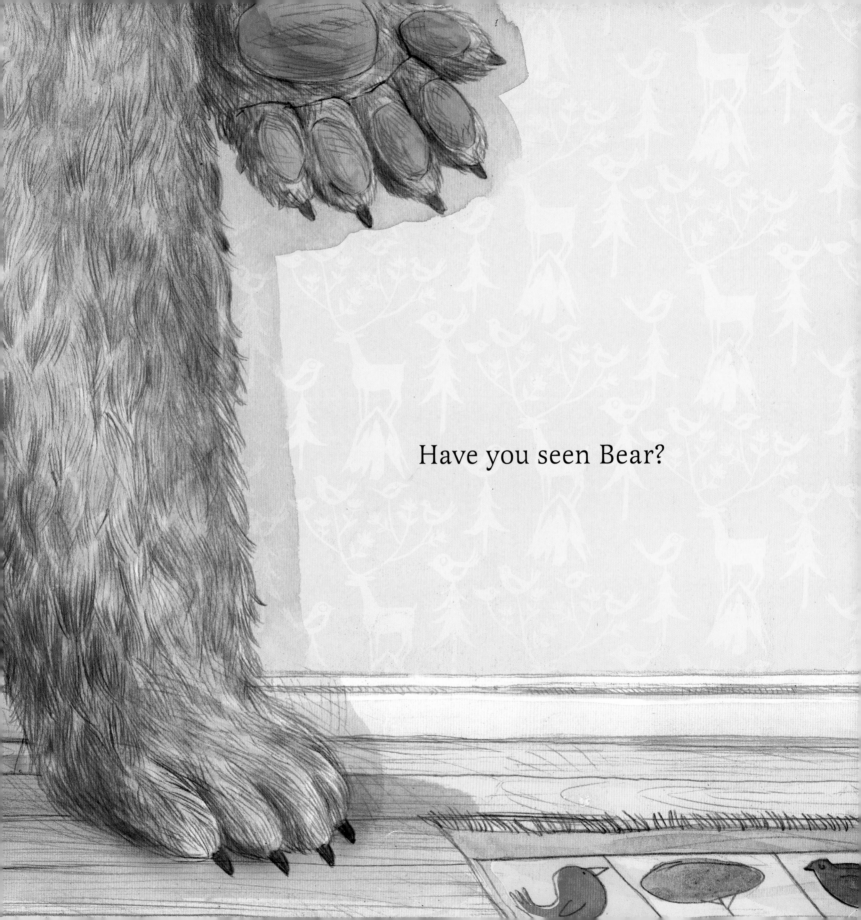

Have you seen Bear?

What? Where?

Where is Bear?

Oh, there is Bear!

I found him, Theodore.
Here is Bear.